Ghost Horse

Emily got out of bed. She ran to the window and pulled back the curtains. In the moonlight, she could see the beautiful white horse!

Emily pinched herself. "Ouch!" Now she knew she wasn't dreaming. The beautiful white horse was really there!

He started walking toward her window. But the closer he got, the paler he got.

Emily gasped. *She could see through the horse!*

Ghost Horse

by **George Edward Stanley**
illustrated by **Ann Barrow**

A STEPPING STONE BOOK™
Random House 🏠 New York

Text copyright © 2000 by George Edward Stanley
Interior illustrations copyright © 2000 by Ann Barrow
Cover illustration copyright © 2009 by Greg Call

All rights reserved. Published in the United States by Random House Children's Books, a division of Random House, Inc., New York.

Random House and the colophon are registered trademarks and A Stepping Stone Book and the colophon are trademarks of Random House, Inc.

Visit us on the Web!
www.randomhouse.com/kids

Educators and librarians, for a variety of teaching tools, visit us at
www.randomhouse.com/teachers

The Library of Congress has cataloged the original edition of this work as follows:
Stanley, George Edward.
Ghost horse / by George Edward Stanley ; illustrated by Ann Barrow. —
1st Random House ed.
    p. cm.
"A Stepping Stone book"
Summary: A ghost horse helps Emily get over her unhappiness when she has to move to a small town, attend a new school, and try to make friends.
ISBN 978-0-307-26500-5 (pbk.) — ISBN 978-0-307-46500-9 (lib. bdg.)
[1. Ghosts—Fiction. 2. Horses—Fiction. 3. Friendship—Fiction.
4. Schools—Fiction. 5. Moving—Fiction.]
I. Barrow, Ann, ill. II. Title.
PZ7.S78694Gh 2004   [Fic]—dc21   2003005189

Printed in the United States of America
17 16 15 14 13 12 11 10 9 8

*To J.D., who believes . . .
and, as always, to Gwen, Charles,
James, and Tambye,
with all my love
—G.E.S.*

*To my parents
—A.B.*

Contents

1
A Nighttime Surprise

Emily Clark opened her eyes. She thought she heard a sound in her room. She held her breath and listened carefully.

But there was only the ticking of her bedside clock. *Was I dreaming?* she wondered.

Emily pulled the covers up over her head. She didn't like her new room in her new house in Westville. She wished she were back in her old room in her old house in Carver City.

Emily heard the sound again. But it wasn't in her room. It came from the backyard.

She sat up in bed. Where had she heard that sound before?

Then she remembered.

"It's a whinny!" she cried. But what was a horse doing in her backyard?

Emily knew their new house had once been a farmhouse. She knew there were almost always horses on farms. *Maybe one of them is still here!* she decided.

Emily got out of bed. She went to her window and pulled back the curtains.

The moon lit up the whole backyard. Emily could see that there was no horse there. But the whinny sound had seemed so real.

Emily sighed. It was probably the wind.

But just as she started to turn away from the window, a white horse walked out from behind a tree. Emily gasped. "I did hear a horse!" she cried.

The horse seemed to glow in the moonlight. He was the most beautiful horse Emily had ever seen.

He walked slowly around the backyard. He made one complete circle, then he stopped.

The horse looked toward Emily's window. He pawed the ground and snorted. He reared up on his hind legs and whinnied some more.

Emily could feel her heart pounding. *Maybe this horse is a surprise for me,* she thought.

Her parents knew she was unhappy about moving. Maybe they bought her a horse to make her happy. Emily was sure that was what had happened. Well, it worked! She was happy now!

She raised her window. If she called to the horse, maybe he would come to her.

Suddenly, the horse started walking away.

"Please don't go!" Emily cried.

The horse turned its head to look right at her.

And then, the horse disappeared!

2

The Worst Day Ever

"Emily! Get up!" her mother called. "We'll both be late if you don't hurry!"

Emily opened her eyes and yawned. Right away, she remembered the beautiful white horse.

She jumped out of bed and went to the window. She pulled back the curtains. The sun was shining brightly, but Emily didn't see the beautiful white horse anywhere in the backyard.

Then she remembered how the horse

had just disappeared. *I must have been dreaming*, she thought.

She got back into bed. She wished she could stay there all day. Today was her first day at her new school.

Emily sat in the car. She didn't want to get out.

"You can't sit here forever," her mother said. "Sooner or later, you'll have to go inside."

Emily looked out the window. She bit her lower lip. All the other kids were riding bicycles to school.

Emily had never learned how to ride a bicycle. No one rode bikes to school in Carver City. The streets were too dangerous.

Suddenly, she was really mad. Why did they have to move to Westville in the first place? It was such a small town.

"Emily, sweetheart, I can't stay here all morning," her mother said. "I'll be late to the office."

Emily knew that tone of voice. Her mother was getting annoyed. In a minute, she wouldn't be asking nicely. She would be telling Emily what would happen if she didn't get out of the car and go into the school building.

Emily opened the door and got out.

"I'll be here to pick you up after school," her mother told her.

"Okay," Emily said.

She tried to sound sad. She hoped her mother would feel sorry for her. She hoped her mother would lean out the window and tell her that she didn't have to go to the new school after all.

Emily started walking slowly away from the car. Her mother didn't say anything. Emily kept getting farther and farther away from the car. She kept getting closer and closer to the front door of the school. Her mother still didn't say anything.

Emily heard the sound she had been dreading. Her mother put the car in gear and drove away from the curb.

Emily could feel the tears welling up in her eyes. Then she saw a girl coming toward her.

Emily turned around quickly. She pretended to wave to her mother while she quickly wiped away the tears on the sleeve of her shirt. She turned back around.

"Hi! I'm Julie!" the girl said. "You're Emily! You're the new girl in our class."

Emily swallowed the lump in her throat. "How did you know my name?" she asked.

"I know everything that goes on in Westville. I've lived here all my life," Julie said. "I saw you through the window. I told Mrs. Benson that you looked lost. Mrs. Benson is our teacher. She told me to come get you."

"Thanks," Emily said.

She followed Julie through the front door of her new school. Julie bounced down the hallway. Emily didn't feel like bouncing.

When they got to the classroom, Emily followed Julie inside.

"Welcome, Emily," Mrs. Benson said.

She turned to the class. "This is Emily Clark. She just moved to our town."

The class all said, "Hello, Emily."

Emily tried to smile.

Then Mrs. Benson showed Emily to her seat.

"I thought you'd like to sit next to Julie," Mrs. Benson said. "She lives only two blocks from you."

Mrs. Benson turned to the rest of the class. "You may all talk quietly until the second bell rings," she added as she started writing on the chalkboard.

"I'll show you my new bicycle at recess," Julie said. She gave Emily a puzzled look. "Why didn't you ride yours to school?"

"I don't have a bike," Emily said.

Julie looked shocked. "You don't?"

"No, I don't." Emily tried to sound bored by the idea.

"I don't know how you'll get around in Westville if you don't have a bicycle to ride," Julie said.

Emily suddenly realized that everyone had stopped talking. They were all staring at her.

She felt like crawling into a hole.

All of a sudden, she remembered the dream she had. She took a deep breath and looked Julie in the eye.

"My parents think bicycles are too dangerous," she said. "That's why they bought me a horse."

3
It's Not a Dream

Emily was glad when the final bell rang.

She picked up her book bag and hurried out of the classroom. She was so miserable that she didn't even say good-bye to Julie.

All day long she had to answer questions about her horse. What kind is it? What color is it? What's its name? What do you wear when you're riding it?

Emily kept making up things.

14

After a while, she forgot what she had said and what she hadn't said. Several times, different kids had to correct her.

What made it even worse was that Julie knew everything there was to know about horses.

"I'd really rather have a horse than a bicycle," Julie had whispered to her at lunch. "I can hardly wait to see yours."

Emily's mother was parked in front of the school. Emily ran down the sidewalk and got into the car.

"Hurry!" she said.

Her mother pulled away from the curb. "Is there anything wrong?" she asked.

"No!" Emily snapped. "I just want to go home."

Emily leaned back in her seat and

sighed. Why did she have to go and tell Julie that she had a horse? Now everybody wanted to see it. Now everybody wanted to ride it.

There was no way she could ever go back to that school again!

Her mother pulled into their driveway and stopped the car. "Are you sure there's nothing wrong?" she asked again.

Emily turned to her. "Could I get a horse?" she asked.

Her mother blinked. "A *horse?*"

Emily nodded.

"We don't have anyplace to keep a horse," her mother said.

"We've got a big backyard," Emily said. "We could keep it there."

"I don't think so, Emily," her mother

said. She opened the car door and got out.

Emily followed slowly.

When she got to her room, she looked out the window. They really did have a big backyard. That was why her parents had bought this house. She wondered if there had ever been a beautiful white horse here when her house was on a farm.

The rest of the afternoon dragged by.

After dinner, Emily decided to ask her father if she could get a horse. He said no, too. So Emily watched her favorite TV show in silence.

Right before she went to bed, Emily's father said she could call one of her friends in Carver City. She chose JoAnn.

JoAnn wanted to know all about her new school. Emily tried to make it sound really awful, but she decided to leave out the part about the horse. She was too embarrassed.

Finally, her father told her it was time to hang up. She and JoAnn promised to call each other every day until Emily could convince her parents to move back to Carver City.

Then Emily went to bed. *I hope I dream about the beautiful white horse,* she thought as she closed her eyes.

There were so many things she would do if she had a horse. She would feed him carrots and sugar cubes. She would ride him to school every day.

The horse would love Emily very much. He would whinny whenever he saw her.

He would whinny...

He would whinny...

He would whinny...

Emily opened her eyes. She was sure that she had heard the whinny sound again. She sat up and listened carefully.

Yes! There it was!

She got out of bed. She ran to the window and pulled back the curtains. In the moonlight, she could see the beautiful white horse!

Emily pinched herself. "Ouch!" Now she knew she wasn't dreaming. The beautiful white horse was really there!

He started walking toward her window. But the closer he got, the paler he got.

Emily gasped. She could see through the horse!

"You're...you're a ghost!" she whispered.

4
The Ghost Horse

Emily jumped back from the window.

Then the most amazing thing happened. The ghost horse stuck his head through the wall of her room!

Emily's eyes went wide. "How did you do that?" she said.

The ghost horse whinnied softly.

Of course! Emily realized. If a *human* ghost could come through a wall, why couldn't a *horse* ghost do the same thing?

Emily swallowed hard. She couldn't

believe this was actually happening.

The rest of the ghost horse came through the wall, filling the room with a soft white glow.

Emily could feel her heart pounding. "Hi," she whispered. "How are you tonight?"

The ghost horse looked at Emily and snorted. But Emily thought it sounded like a nice snort.

She started walking slowly toward the ghost horse. She didn't want to scare him. "You are so beautiful," she said. She reached out her hand to pat him on the nose.

The ghost horse stepped back shyly.

"Don't be afraid," Emily said softly. "I won't hurt you."

She reached out her hand again. This

time, the ghost horse let Emily pat his nose. It was so soft.

Emily wished the ghost horse could talk. Why had he come to her?

The ghost horse knelt down on his front legs.

"Do you want me to get on?" Emily asked.

The ghost horse whinnied softly.

"Okay," Emily said.

She took hold of the ghost horse's mane. She swung her right leg over his back and climbed on.

Then she took a deep breath. She tried not to think about the fact that she was sitting on a ghost.

The ghost horse stood up and started walking toward the wall. Emily wondered what would happen to her when the ghost horse went back through it. She held on tight.

The ghost horse's head went through the wall. Emily closed her eyes. She was sure her head would hit the wall. She was sure she would fall off the ghost horse.

Emily felt a cool breeze on her face. She opened her eyes. She and the ghost horse were in the backyard. Emily had gone through the wall, too!

They passed under the trees and went through the wooden back fence. Now they were in the alley behind her house.

Where is he taking me? Emily wondered.

The ghost horse started to trot. Emily held tighter to his mane.

When they reached the end of the alley, the ghost horse galloped into the middle

of the street and started racing through Westville. The streetlights became blurs.

Emily closed her eyes and held on for dear life.

When she opened her eyes again, they were no longer in town. For the first time, Emily began to feel scared.

After a few minutes, the ghost horse stopped galloping. He slowed to a trot. Then he slowed to a walk.

Finally, he turned off the road and started up a narrow path.

In the moonlight, Emily could see a large metal gate. Beyond the metal gate, Emily could see a lot of tombstones.

"Oh, no!" she cried.

The ghost horse had taken her to a cemetery!

5
The Secret in the Cemetery

The ghost horse walked through the metal gate and started down a narrow path.

He twisted and turned between big old tombstones, taking Emily deeper and deeper into the cemetery.

The tree branches looked like long arms as they swayed back and forth in the wind. Emily was sure that any minute they would grab her and pull her from the ghost horse.

Mist floated out from the shadows and danced around her face.

Emily shivered. She had never been in a cemetery after dark before. She didn't like it at all.

Finally, the ghost horse stopped and knelt down. Emily slowly got off.

Was he going to leave her in the middle of a cemetery?

The ghost horse stood up, but didn't run away. Instead, he lifted his left hoof and touched a tombstone.

Emily bent down to look. She was glad the moon was bright. It was easy to read the names.

MARY WIKKENS   JOHN WIKKENS
1925-1957   1923-1957

"Who are these people?" Emily asked the ghost horse.

The ghost horse whinnied softly. Emily was sure he was trying to tell her something. *But what?* she wondered.

6
The New Librarian

When Emily got to school the next morning, she felt like she was walking around in a dream. She still couldn't believe what had happened the night before.

When the kids asked her again about her horse, she said, "I rode him last night! It was a lot of fun!"

It came out of her mouth before she could stop it.

Most of the kids believed her. But a

few of them acted like they didn't.

"Did you really ride him after dark?" Julie whispered to her during recess.

Emily nodded. Suddenly, she had a great idea. "I'll show him to you. I'll ride over to your house tonight."

Emily just hoped she was telling Julie the truth this time.

That night, the ghost horse stuck his head through Emily's bedroom wall again and whinnied softly.

"I knew you'd come back!" Emily said sleepily.

She got out of bed and climbed onto the ghost horse's back. "We're going to my friend Julie's house," she said. She gently pulled the ghost horse's mane to the left, and they rode through the wall of her room.

When they reached Julie's house, Emily pulled the ghost horse to a stop.

How can I let Julie know I'm here? Emily wondered.

It was too late to ring the doorbell. That would probably make Julie's parents really mad.

Emily finally decided just to ride the ghost horse through the front door.

"Don't whinny now," Emily warned him.

Emily guided the ghost horse up the front step and closed her eyes. When she opened them, she was inside Julie's house.

She rode through the living room and the dining room and the kitchen. When she reached the back of the house, she saw three closed doors.

One of these rooms has to be Julie's bedroom, she thought, looking around. *But which one is it?*

Emily guided the ghost horse toward the first door.

This time she kept her eyes open. It was incredible. One minute she was looking at a door. The next minute she was inside a room. She didn't feel a thing when she went through the door.

Unfortunately, the first room was a bathroom. It was so small that the ghost horse had to back his way out.

They went through the second door.

Emily saw a man and a woman. They were both snoring. *Oh, no!* she thought. *Julie's parents!* She quickly guided the ghost horse out of that room.

Finally, they went through the third door. There was a night-light on inside the room. Julie was asleep in her bed.

The ghost horse knelt down, and Emily got off. She shook Julie's shoulder.

Julie groaned and opened her eyes. "Emily! What are you doing here? How did you get into my house?"

"We came through your front door," Emily said. "I forgot to tell you that my horse is a ghost horse."

"A *ghost* horse?" Julie cried. She sat up in bed.

Emily nodded. "He's like a regular

horse except that he's a ghost. But my parents really didn't buy him. He just comes to see me every night."

Julie gasped.

"What's wrong?" Emily asked.

"When I was little, my grandmother used to tell me stories about a ghost horse that walked around your house late at night," Julie said. "I thought she was just making them up."

Emily shook her head. "No, Julie, she wasn't. The ghost horse is real."

Julie reached out and patted the ghost horse's nose. "He's so beautiful," she said.

"You're not mad because he's a ghost horse?" Emily asked.

"Oh, no!" Julie said. She got out of bed and shyly hugged the ghost horse's neck.

"I don't care what kind of horse he is."

"But what am I going to tell the other kids at school?" Emily asked.

"He's still a horse, Emily," Julie said. "You don't have to tell them that he's a ghost horse."

"That's true," Emily said.

"And maybe one of these days you'll get a real horse," Julie added. "Then you won't have to worry about it."

Emily was sure that would never happen, but she didn't say so.

"Julie, do you know who John and Mary Wikkens are?" she asked.

"No," Julie said. She patted the ghost horse's nose again. "Why?"

"They're buried in the cemetery here. I think the ghost horse knows them,"

Emily said. "He took me there last night."

"He did?" Julie asked.

Emily nodded. "I think he's trying to tell me something," she said. "I hoped you could help me figure it out."

Julie thought for a minute. "Wait! There's a Ms. Wikkens at our school!" she said. "She's the new librarian."

"I wonder if those people in the cemetery were her parents?" Emily said.

"We can ask her tomorrow," Julie said.

The ghost horse whinnied softly. He shifted from one foot to the other.

"I think he wants to leave now," Emily said. "I'll see you at school in the morning."

"Okay," Julie said. "Thank you for showing me your horse."

When Emily and the ghost horse got back to her room, she patted him softly on his side.

"We'll find out something tomorrow for sure," she told him. "I promise."

7
Moonlight's Story

"Hurry, Mom!" Emily cried. "I want to get to school early!"

"I'm hurrying," her mother said. She backed the car out of the driveway and started down the street.

"Why the rush?" her mother asked. "You weren't this excited about school before."

"I have to meet my new friend, Julie," Emily explained. "And I don't want to be late!"

"Well, I can't drive any faster," her mother said.

Finally, they reached the school.

Emily jumped out of the car and ran to the front door. Julie was waiting for her.

"We have five minutes to talk to Ms. Wikkens before the first bell rings," Julie said.

They hurried down the hallway and turned a corner. The door to the library was open. Emily followed Julie inside.

"Hi, Ms. Wikkens," Julie said.

Ms. Wikkens looked up from her computer. She had the whitest hair Emily had ever seen. "Good morning, Julie," she said.

"This is Emily," Julie told her. "She just moved here."

"Hello, Emily. Welcome to our school."

Ms. Wikkens gave Emily a big, friendly smile. It made her blue eyes sparkle.

Emily knew right away that Ms. Wikkens was a grown-up who would listen to them. "Hello," she said.

"Can we talk to you?" Julie asked. "It's very important."

"Okay," Ms. Wikkens said. She pulled her chair over to a big table. "Let's sit here."

Julie and Emily sat down at the table.

"Who wants to go first?" Ms. Wikkens said.

Julie nudged Emily. "Ask her," she said.

Emily gulped. She had hoped Julie would do all the talking. Now Ms. Wikkens was looking at her. Emily took a deep breath. "Are your parents buried in that cemetery outside of town?" she asked.

Ms. Wikkens blinked in surprise. "Yes," she said. "But how did you know that?"

"Emily's horse took her there the other night," Julie said.

"*Emily's horse?* I don't understand," Ms. Wikkens said. "What are you talking about?"

Julie looked over at Emily. "Can I tell her?"

Emily nodded.

"Emily has a ghost horse," Julie explained.

Ms. Wikkens smiled at them. "A *ghost* horse?"

"Yes," Julie said. "He comes to see her every night."

Ms. Wikkens shook her head. "That's

47

impossible, girls. Ghosts aren't real."

"Well, this one is," Julie said. "I've seen him, too."

"He showed me your parents' graves, Ms. Wikkens. I think he knows them," Emily said. "He's white, and he glows at night. He's really beautiful."

Now Ms. Wikkens's eyes were big and wide. She wasn't smiling that grown-up smile anymore. "Where do you live, Emily?" she asked.

"I live at 1016 Brice Street," Emily said.

Ms. Wikkens gasped. "It just can't be!" She had tears in her eyes. "That's my horse! That's Moonlight!"

Ms. Wikkens was quiet for a minute. Then she began to explain. "It happened a long time ago when I was about your

age. My family lived where Emily lives now. It was still a farm then. I begged and begged my parents to buy me a horse for my birthday. Finally, they did. I named him Moonlight, because he glowed in the moonlight." Ms. Wikkens took a deep breath.

"One night, there was a fire in the barn. Moonlight was trapped. My parents tried to save him, but they couldn't. Moonlight died in the fire." She looked down at the table.

"Then everything went bad. A few months later, both my parents died in an accident. I went to live with an aunt. I only moved back to Westville a couple of months ago. I was gone for forty years."

Ms. Wikkens wiped the tears from her eyes. "Emily, Julie, my head says there are no ghosts," she said, "but my heart wants it to be true. I would love to see Moonlight again."

Emily thought about it for a minute. The first bell rang. She had to decide fast.

"Tell me where you live," she said. "Moonlight and I will ride over to your house tonight."

8
The Search Is Over

Emily and Julie hurried out of the library. They got to their classroom before the second bell rang. Mrs. Benson was writing on the chalkboard.

Emily walked slowly to her seat. She had a terrible thought. When she went over to Ms. Wikkens's house tonight, Moonlight would probably want to stay there. He wouldn't come to Emily's room anymore. She wouldn't have a horse at all!

Emily was happy for Ms. Wikkens, but she was sad for herself.

Several times during the day, Mrs. Benson had to scold her for not paying attention.

Finally, school was over. Emily was so happy to go home.

Emily went straight to her room and lay down on her bed. She felt like crying, but she knew it wouldn't do any good.

She went to the kitchen. She ate a snack and did her homework.

After dinner, her father took them all to get ice cream cones. Emily only ate half of hers.

Emily went to bed right when they got back. She turned out her light, but she couldn't go to sleep. She lay in bed thinking about Moonlight.

Emily opened her eyes. She had fallen asleep after all. What if Moonlight had come and she had missed him?

All of a sudden, she heard Moonlight's whinny.

"Moonlight!" she cried.

Moonlight stuck his head through the wall of her room. He seemed excited about something. Emily was sure she knew what it was, too!

"You're wondering how I know your name, aren't you?"

Moonlight whinnied again.

"We're going to see a friend of yours," Emily whispered into his ear.

She climbed onto Moonlight's back, and they rode through the wall of her room. When they reached the street, Emily headed toward Ms. Wikkens's house.

Ms. Wikkens had left the front porch light on. Emily guided Moonlight up the sidewalk. She could tell that Moonlight was getting even more excited.

When they rode through the front door, they were in the living room. Ms. Wikkens was asleep in a chair. Moonlight whinnied softly.

Ms. Wikkens opened her eyes. She stood up. "Moonlight!" she cried. "I thought I'd never see you again!"

9
Moonlight's Last Ride

"You ride in front," Emily said. "After all, Moonlight is your horse."

Ms. Wikkens got on Moonlight. Emily sat behind her and put her arms around Ms. Wikkens's waist.

Ms. Wikkens made a clicking sound with her tongue. "Let's go, Moonlight!" she cried.

Moonlight trotted through the front door of Ms. Wikkens's house and out into the street.

"Where are we going?" Emily asked.

"To Moonlight's favorite spot," Ms. Wikkens said. She gently prodded Moonlight's flank.

Moonlight started galloping down the street.

"Faster, Moonlight, faster!" Ms. Wikkens cried.

Before long, they were out of town and racing through the countryside.

Emily saw a wooden fence ahead of them.

"Watch this!" Ms. Wikkens said.

When Moonlight reached the fence, he didn't go through it. He jumped over it. For a few seconds, they were flying through the air. Then Moonlight landed in stride, and they headed toward a line of trees.

"There's the river, Emily!" Ms. Wikkens pointed through the trees.

When they reached its bank, Moonlight stopped.

"Why did we come here?" Emily asked.

"Moonlight loved this place when he was alive," Ms. Wikkens said. "He liked to drink from the river."

Emily and Ms. Wikkens sat down under a tree.

"Ms. Wikkens, why did Moonlight come to my house?" Emily asked.

"I guess he was looking for me," Ms. Wikkens said.

"Really?" said Emily.

Ms. Wikkens shrugged. "He knew where my parents were, because he's buried in the pasture just beyond them. But he didn't know where I was."

"What will happen to him now?" Emily asked.

For a few minutes, Ms. Wikkens didn't say anything. Emily could see tears on her cheeks.

"He's been looking for me for a long time, Emily," she finally answered. "Now he knows I'm all right. I have a feeling he won't be back."

"You mean he'll never come to *anybody's* house again?" Emily asked.

Ms. Wikkens shook her head sadly.

Emily sighed. "I told all the kids at school that I had a horse. They thought I meant a real horse. Now I won't even have a ghost horse."

Ms. Wikkens wiped her tears away. "I'm sorry, Emily," she said. "I wish there were something I could do about that."

"It's all right," Emily said. "I shouldn't have lied to them."

"We'd better go," Ms. Wikkens said. She whistled for Moonlight.

Moonlight stopped drinking and looked up. Ms. Wikkens made the clicking sound again. Moonlight came over to her and knelt down.

"You ride in front this time," Ms. Wikkens said.

Emily got on. Ms. Wikkens got on behind her.

Moonlight raced through the trees. He raced through the fields. He jumped over the wooden fence again. Finally, they were back in Westville.

Moonlight took Ms. Wikkens to her house. "I love you, Moonlight. Thank you for waiting for me all these years," she said. "Now please take Emily home."

When they reached Emily's house, Moonlight went through the wall of her room, and Emily got off. She hugged Moonlight's neck.

"I love you, too, Moonlight," she said.

Moonlight whinnied softly. Then he turned slowly and disappeared through the wall of Emily's room.

10

A Real Horse

"Emily! Get up!" her mother called. "We'll both be late if you don't hurry!"

Emily sat up in bed and yawned.

A week had gone by since her ride with Ms. Wikkens. Every night she'd waited for Moonlight. But Ms. Wikkens was right. Moonlight never came back.

The kids at school had stopped asking about her horse. She knew they no longer believed her.

"Hurry, Emily!" her mother called

again. "I'm supposed to make sure you're at school early!"

That's strange, Emily thought.

Emily ate her breakfast and brushed her teeth, then she dressed as fast as she could.

It only took them a few minutes to get to school. Her mother stopped in front. Emily looked out the window and gasped.

Julie and all the other kids in her class were standing together on the playground. Ms. Wikkens was with them. She was holding the reins of a beautiful white horse.

Emily looked at her mother.

"It's Ms. Wikkens's new horse," her mother said. "She called me one day last week. It was the strangest conversation I've ever had. She said she had a lot to thank you for." Emily's mother looked at her. "What did she mean?"

Emily shrugged. "Did she say anything else?"

"Yes. She said you could name the horse. And that you could ride it anytime you wanted."

"Do you think she'll let me ride it to school?" Emily asked.

"Why would you want to ride a horse to school when you could ride your bicycle?" her mother asked.

"My bicycle?" Emily cried.

Her mother smiled. "We're going to buy you one today. Your father said he'd teach you how to ride it so you can bike to school."

Emily hugged her mother's neck. "Thank you! Thank you!" she said.

Emily got out of the car and ran over to where Ms. Wikkens and the horse were standing next to all the bicycles.

"Do I really get to name him?" Emily asked.

Ms. Wikkens nodded.

"Then I'm going to call him Moonlight," Emily said.

Ms. Wikkens smiled. "I think that's a wonderful name, Emily," she said.

About the Author

Although George Stanley has never seen a ghost horse, he did think he once saw a ghost dog! On Christmas night, he was awakened by the family's yellow lab, Daisy. Daisy was surrounded by an eerie blue light. He soon found out the dog wasn't a ghost at all—the sweater she'd received for Christmas glowed in the dark!

George Stanley has written over fifty books for young people, several of them award winners. He and his wife, Gwen, live in Lawton, Oklahoma. They have two sons, Charles and James, and a daughter-in-law, Tambye.

Do you like books about animals?
You may also want to read

Absolutely Lucy

Bobby's mother smiled. "Now it's time for your special present," she said.

His father said, "Close your eyes."

Bobby was glad to close his eyes. It would be easier to look surprised when he opened them.

"Okay, Bobby," his father called, "you can look!"

Bobby opened his eyes. He didn't have to pretend to be surprised. Or happy. In his father's arms was a puppy. The cutest, squirmiest little dog Bobby had ever seen.